Phoebe's Fabulous Father

LOUISA CAMPBELL

Illustrated by
BRIDGET STARR TAYLOR

Harcourt Brace & Company
SAN DIEGO   NEW YORK   LONDON

Requests for permission to make copies of any part of the work should be mailed to:
Permissions Department, Harcourt Brace & Company, 6277 Sea Harbor Drive,
Orlando, Florida 32887-6777.
Library of Congress Cataloging-in-Publication Data
Campbell, Louisa.
Phoebe's fabulous father/Louisa Campbell; illustrated by Bridget Starr Taylor.—1st ed.
p.   cm.
Summary: As she and her mother run errands around town before the family's
big concert, a young girl comes to realize how special her father is.
ISBN 0-15-200996-5
[1. Family life—Fiction. 2. Musicians—Fiction. 3. Fathers and daughters—Fiction.
4. Dinosaurs—Fiction.] I. Taylor, Bridget Starr, 1959-   ill. II. Title.
PZ7.C15515Ph   1996
[E]—dc20   95-34811

First edition
F E D C B A
PRINTED IN SINGAPORE

The illustrations in this book were done in chalk pastels and acrylics on paper.
The display type was hand-lettered by Judythe Sieck.
The text type was set in Phaistos Bold with Phalanx initial capitals.
Color separations by Bright Arts, Ltd. Singapore
Printed and bound by Tien Wah Press, Singapore
This book was printed with soya-based inks on Leykam recycled paper, which contains
more than 20 percent postconsumer waste and has a total recycled content of at least 50 percent.
Production supervision by Warren Wallerstein and Pascha Gerlinger
Designed by Judythe Sieck

With love, to my fabulous
mother and father —L. C.

To John, for making this
and so much else possible —B. S. T.

Cloud Valley

It was Saturday morning and time to run errands. Phoebe rode on the back of her mom's bike. "Fly, Mommy, fly!" sang Phoebe. It was just the two of them. Dad was at home practicing.

"Off we go!" said Mom. They swooshed down the hill to town.

"Wheeeeeeee!" yelled Phoebe as she tossed her head back in the sweet breeze.

First stop was Lola's Laundromat. Phoebe helped her mom bring in a load of dirty clothes.

Lola the laundress pointed with her chin and said, "See! There's your party dress—washed and starched!"

"Hurray!" shouted Phoebe. "We have a concert tonight."

"You're darn tooting," said Lola. "I've got tickets."

Phoebe and her parents were musicians. Phoebe played the violin, Mom played the viola, and Dad, the cello.

"Toodle-loo!" said Mom. She whisked her daughter out the door.

Next stop was the fruit stand. Phoebe pointed and said, "I want a giant melon for my giant daddy!"

Dad was having problems with the music for tonight. Phoebe and her mom knew his playing would be fine, but Dad insisted that it be perfect. Sometimes Phoebe felt sorry for her dad because he was always working. Other times she felt angry.

Mom made her voice low and gravelly to sound like Dad's. "I must eat something strengthening before the concert."

"Silly Mommy! That's what Daddy always says!" shouted Phoebe. "And I want an alligator pear for me, please!"

"In a while, crocodile," answered Mom.

Back on the bike Phoebe said, "I bet Daddy will forget to iron his tux for the concert!"

"No doubt," answered Mom. She smiled and shook her head. "We need to take care of him. Remember, little one, he takes care of us, too."

Phoebe sighed. She guessed her mom was right, but sometimes Phoebe did wish that her dad was different. Why couldn't he be more like other dads? Other dads did *other things* besides *work*. Kate and her dad went boating every Saturday. Luke and his father liked to fish. Eleanor and Emily's dad took them riding on his motorcycle. But it seemed like all Phoebe's dad did was play the cello and play the cello some more.

Mom braked the bike and Phoebe left her thoughts behind. They swooped into the shoe repair.

"My daddy's shoes are worn-out again," said Phoebe.

"He should buy himself a new pair," said Mom, "but such colossal shoes are hard to find!"

"Not to worry," said Mrs. Falcone. "We'll fix this pair up good as new. Won't we now, Freddy?" She gave her husband a nudge. "Give Mrs. Saurus her pumps. She'll need them tonight."

"Thank you much," said Mom. "Cheerio!" She and Phoebe zipped out the door.

In the grocery Mr. Sammy said, "Well now, ladies! How about some big fish this morning?"

"Big fish are my favorite," said Phoebe.

"They're firm and juicy!" added the butcher.

"Wonderful," said Phoebe's mom. "We'll take four."

"Coming right up!" Mr. Sammy wrapped the fish in white paper and tied them with string.

"Today's a concert day!" explained Phoebe. "I'm extra hungry."

Mr. Sammy gave Phoebe a slice of bologna to nibble.

"*Mmm, mmm!*" hummed Phoebe. "Thanks!" *Chomp-chomp.*

"Bye now!" said Mom. She grabbed the fish and took Phoebe's hand. They slogged through the sawdust and out the door.

The air inside Twin Bakery smelled sweet and buttery.

"Greetings, friends," said Terry, one of the twins. "You're in for a treat today! We've some lovely loaves, coarse and chewy, just the way y'all like 'em."

"Fine," said Mom. "Give us a dozen!"

"My pleasure!" Terry chuckled. "Now, dears, have a donut. This batch is particularly scrumptious, if I do say so myself."

"Yum, yum!" said Mom, munching on her donut.

"I WANT ICE CREAM!" declared Phoebe.

"Phoebe!" scolded Mom.

"There, there," said Terry. *"Ciao."* He tickled Phoebe under the chin.

"Thanks!" said Mom. "Ta-ta!"

Mom pedaled a loop-the-loop over to the Ice Cream Palace. "You may have a cone, Phoebe, if you promise to be more polite," she said.

"But you always say that I'm a little monster," argued Phoebe.

"Yes, but I don't see why you can't be a *polite* little monster." Mom jingled change out of her purse into Phoebe's palm. "*Tsk, tsk.*"

"I want a dinosaur-double-dip, *please!*" said Phoebe and smacked her lips.

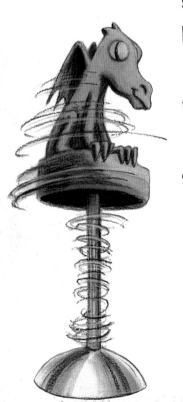

ack across the river was Heaney's Drug Store. Inside, Phoebe hopped onto her favorite stool for a spin.

At the Griffin cologne counter Mr. Heaney said, "Not you two again! Why, you just purchased a megasize bottle last week!"

"Daddy used it all up," announced Phoebe. "Mommy says he slathers it on. He says it's for luck." Phoebe stopped spinning and took a breath. "Before concerts, Mommy dabs a tiny bit behind my ears, too!"

"*Ho, ho,*" laughed Mr. Heaney. He sold them another huge bottle of the deluxe scent. Mr. Heaney winked. "Break a leg tonight."

"Thanks a million," said Mom. "See you in the funnies!" The pair darted out the door.

In the music store the metronome echoed *tick-tock*. "HI!" said Phoebe. "I need my daddy's heavy-duty strings. There's a concert tonight."

"Of course!" said Miss Esther, who owned the store. "I wouldn't miss it for the world!" She patted a waxed paper package. "Soon we'll need to order heavy-duty strings for *you*, little Phoebe!"

"Good! Then I'll be *BIG* Phoebe."

"We're running late!" Mom snatched the package, paid, and snapped her pocketbook shut. "Much obliged! Bye, now!"

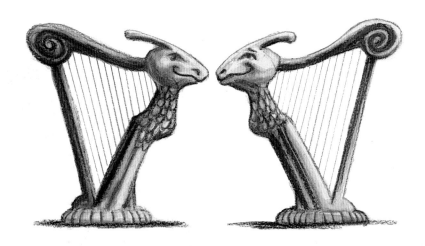

Before getting back on the bike, Phoebe and her mom popped into the library to drop off a book. Phoebe raced up to the listening ledge. She pulled an old album from the rack. The cover read: EDDIE SAURUS PLAYS J. S. REX, *THE FOSSIL CELLO SUITES*.

"Mommy!" screeched Phoebe. "Come quick! It's a record by Daddy."

"Oh, yes. I'd forgotten about that—it's a fabulous album. It's one from before you were born, when your dad was a soloist. In those days your dad was always on the go. He was world-famous."

They listened to the record and Phoebe asked, "Why isn't Daddy a world-famous soloist anymore?"

"Because he'd rather stay home and play music with us."

"Hmm." Phoebe thought about what her mother said.

In the way out of town Phoebe glanced up at the Concert Hall marquee and the ad for their performance tonight. Phoebe also caught a glimpse of the poster—her Dad looked very handsome.

All of a sudden Phoebe felt proud. "Mommy!" she said. "I love our family!"

Their bike took them swiftly home. Phoebe giggled. She always felt glad the moment she saw their house and she heard the bright sounds of her father's music.

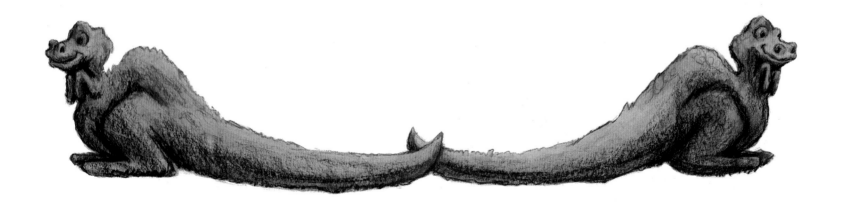

From his tower Dad saw them and rushed outside. "I'm so glad you two are home. The house is empty without you."

"We went everywhere and remembered everything for the concert tonight!" Phoebe shouted, "I love you, Daddy!"

"And I love you, too!" he answered. Then Dad gave her a special little kiss, just as he always did.

"Daddy," Phoebe sang, "you are my very own fabulous father!"